only when the sun shines brightly

Magnus Mills

This edition published in the UK by
acorn book company
PO Box 191
Tadworth
Surrey KT20 5YQ

email: info@acornbook.co.uk

www.acornbook.co.uk

ISBN 0-9544959-3-4

British Library Cataloguing in Publication Data.
A catalogue record for this book is available from the British Library.

Copyright © Magnus Mills, 1999, 2004

First Published 1999

This revised edition first published 2004

Magnus Mills aserts the moral right to be identified as the author of this work.

for Lisa

CONTENTS

the Comforter

I was looking for a way into the cathedral when the archdeacon found me. There were several doors, and I had paused before one of them.

'Locked is it?' he asked, smiling.

'Well, I haven't actually…..er…..not sure really.'

'Probably locked,' he announced. 'Probably far too early. I always arrive far too early.'

The archdeacon laughed in a benevolent way and I smiled.

'You must be the architect,' he beamed.

'I suppose I am,' I replied. 'Yes.'

'Very good. Very pleased you could come. There's a door along here we can try.'

He shepherded me round the corner, past some shrubs and newly emerging bulbs. On this side of the building it was damp and shady, and there was a smaller door. It was locked.

'They're trying to keep us out, I think!' he laughed again. This time it was a compulsory laugh, and I joined in. The archdeacon's face was pink, his eyes were blue, his hair was white. He smiled a lot and took me under his wing. We sat down, side by side, on a wooden bench.

'They always seem to rope me in for these committees,' said the archdeacon, placing his briefcase flat across his knees. 'Probably think it'll keep me out of mischief! They're most probably right!' This time I anticipated the laughter, which seemed to please him.

'Would you like a sandwich?' he asked, opening the lid. 'I'm supposed to keep papers in here, but to tell you the truth I hardly ever get round to reading them. Always get given lots of papers. In case I miss something, I suppose. Good job really. My wife says I never listen. Not properly. Still, it all goes down in the minutes. I'm just there to agree with everyone really. Salmon and cucumber, I think. Yes. Like one?'

I said, 'Thank you, no,' and he turned and smiled with bushy eyebrows raised.

'You don't mind if I....?'

'No, no. Of course not. Bon appetit.'

'Ah, merci.'

The swallows were skimming low and it might rain soon. I could feel the dampness coming through from the bench, but it would be rude of me to rise. So I waited while the archdeacon broke his bread alone. Silence had fallen, for the moment, on our small corner of the world. One of the flagstones between the bench and the door had a crack across it, from which moss grew. Some of the others had signs of weakness, here and there. I began to count them, from left to right, in my head, but the silence had become too much for my companion.

'Lovely garden, don't you think?'

'Yes.'

'Absolutely lovely. Abounds with flowers in summer. There's a man comes from the council, twice a week. Sort of loan, I believe. Do you know him?'

'I'm afraid not.'

'Very nice man. Will always give you the time of day. Very nice. Always sweeps up.'

'That's good,' I said.

'Yes indeed.'

We smiled and nodded together. A moment passed.

'Cost a lot will it?' he asked. 'This new roof?'

'I'm not sure.'

'Can't be helped, I suppose. Nothing lasts forever.'

I glanced at my watch.

'Oh dear,' said the archdeacon, closing his lid and rising quickly. 'Rather damp, this bench.'

Here was the opportunity for me to rise as well, and we paced about upon the flagstones, turning our backs on the breeze that was getting up. The shrubs rustled as the archdeacon fastened his overcoat buttons, an empty briefcase clamped between his knees. In the tower high above a bell struck nine.

'This always happens to me when I arrive early somewhere,' he said, preparing to see the funny side of it. 'I end up being late.'

We waited.

'Aren't there any others?' I asked.

'Should be,' he replied. 'Usually seven or eight at least.'

'Perhaps we should try the front door again.'

'Wasn't it locked?'

'Well, I thought you said it was.'

He pulled a face. 'Oh dear.'

The front door was not locked, but because of the archdeacon, we entered the cathedral late. The rest of the committee were waiting inside, still wearing their coats.

'So sorry,' he explained. 'Slight misunderstanding about which door.'

His arrival brought in the fresh air from outside. They forgave him with a shiver.

'Better late than never, Norman,' said the chairman, leading the way to where an antechamber had been prepared. There was a round table surrounded by wooden chairs with leather seats, and in the corner stood a cylinder-gas heater, pale flames flickering on the gauze. As we looked for our places the archdeacon took command.

'Now I'm going to sit next to you because I know absolutely nothing about architecture!'

He sat down in the Treasurer's seat beside mine, in spite of the card marked 'Treasurer'. The chairman's table plan was now upset. He tried to intervene. The archdeacon did not listen. He was telling me about his pen.

'Gift from the last chancellor. Christmas nineteen seventy two it was. No, sorry, seventy one. Very nice man. Always exchanged gifts at Christmas. Without fail. Terrible loss and we miss him greatly. Never let me down, this pen.'

He removed its cap, examined the nib and then replaced the cap again.

'Won't be needing it today, of course. Not with all these pencils Frank provides. Always a box of pencils. You wouldn't believe it. If I had all the pencils.....oh, we're ready, are we Frank? Sorry.'

The chairman, meanwhile, had made diplomatic moves and managed to rearrange the table plan without the archdeacon even noticing. At last we were all seated and the minutes of the previous meeting were read aloud.

Beside me the archdeacon had fallen silent for the time being. As business proceeded and various points were raised, he carefully balanced his pencil at the edge of his pad. If he placed a finger on one end of the pencil, it would dip and touch the table surface. When he removed his finger it became level again. After half an hour he suddenly took up his pencil and wrote LIGHT BULB in block letters across one corner of the pad. The rest of the time he nodded and smiled, and gave the appearance of listening.

At the end of the first session, the chairman addressed the archdeacon: 'Unless you've got anything to add to that Norman?'

'No, no,' said my neighbour with confidence. 'Sounds fine to me.'

the Comforter

There then followed a welcome break for coffee and biscuits. Before I had a chance to stretch myself, a firm hand took me by the arm and led me over to a newly opened hatch.

As he offered a plate of Malted Milks the archdeacon spoke in a low voice. 'Not going too bad, is it?'

'So far no,' I agreed.

'Not too bad at all. Odd that they haven't mentioned the roof yet.'

'Odd?'

'Yes. Must be a trial for your patience.'

'Why's that?'

'You being the architect and everything.' He looked at me. 'You did say you were the architect didn't you?'

'Yes, architect would be one way of describing me,' I replied. 'I sort of plan things really. Set things up.'

'Oh,' he said. 'I see.'

The archdeacon stirred sugar into his tea before he spoke again. 'But we will be getting onto the roof eventually, won't we?' he asked.

'Eventually,' I said.

When we got back to the committee table the chairman had already been round tidying up. The archdeacon's pencil, for example, had been returned to the holder in the centre of the table. Also the place cards indicating people's status had been rearranged in the new order dictated by the archdeacon's decision to sit next to me. As I resumed my seat I selected a pencil for the second session, and chose one for the archdeacon too.

'How kind,' he remarked, preparing to balance it again at the edge of his pad.

The second session continued in much the same way as the first, with a number of reports being read out and approved. After a while the archdeacon drew a circle around LIGHT BULB, the outline of which he renewed from time to time as the hours passed, until it became a dark ring surrounding the words. Then he added a pair of ears at the top of the circle, as well as some cats' whiskers, before laying his pencil down.

The gas-cylinder heater in the corner had taken the earlier coolness out of the room, and now, humming quietly, it began to devour the remaining fresh air. There were no windows that could be opened for ventilation, and because the walls were thick, few sounds came in from the world outside. Apart from the hourly chiming of the bell in the tower above, the discussions of the committee were all that could be heard.

At one o'clock the chairman announced that it was time for lunch, and the archdeacon immediately got up and headed for the door.

'Where are you going Norman?' asked the chairman.

'Just a little errand I've got to run,' replied the archdeacon.

'Won't be long.'

'But we're having a working lunch. There isn't time for you to go wandering off anywhere.'

The archdeacon looked dismayed. 'I haven't any sandwiches left.'

'You can share mine,' I said.

'Oh,' said the archdeacon, returning to his place. 'Thank you. You're so very kind.'

The other members of the committee all had packed lunches wrapped in silver foil. Some also had apples, while some had individual fruit pies or cakes. My sandwiches were plain cheddar cheese, but there were enough for two.

The archdeacon ate in silence as further conversation was exchanged around the table. Then, before the afternoon session began in earnest, he was permitted a brief stroll around the cathedral close, just to stretch his legs. I offered to accompany him and we went outside.

'I must say,' he confided, as the door swung shut behind us, 'I've never attended such a long meeting before. Seems to be going on forever.'

'Well, there's a lot to cover,' I said.

'Oh yes,' he replied. 'Yes, I can see that. Not that I'm complaining, of course. It's all very interesting.'

'Glad to hear it.'

The sky was dark. It had been raining. Our walk took us across wet flagstones and past the bench where we had sat that morning. We stopped to admire a hydrangea bush about to come into leaf. I glanced at my watch. We went back inside.

At two o'clock we took our seats again, and now some papers were circulated. The archdeacon played a helpful role here, passing the numbered pages around in their correct order, and placing his own in a neat pile before him. It seemed important to him that the corners of the pages should all be exactly lined up with each other, and he spent some considerable time ensuring this was so. After that, there was nothing else for him to do but sit and listen. If his opinion on some issue was asked, he would agree wholeheartedly with the previous speaker, but most of the time he was left to his own devices. Due to the gas-cylinder heater, the air in the room had now become thick and heavy, and the archdeacon was unable to prevent his eyes from occasionally closing. Every now and then I would notice his head nodding slowly forward as he drifted almost to the verge of sleep. Yet he never fully succumbed, and the tap of a pencil or a slight change in the speaker's tone of voice would be enough to snap his eyes wide open again. In this way the afternoon ticked past and gradually gave way to evening. Finally the bell in the tower above struck six and the meeting came to a close.

the Comforter

As the chairman gathered up some papers he looked over the rim of his glasses at the yawning archdeacon.

'Now don't forget Norman. Bright and early tomorrow morning,' he said.

A puzzled look crossed the archdeacon's face.

'Tomorrow?' he asked.

'Of course,' replied the chairman.

'But I had no idea we were meeting tomorrow.'

The room had become very quite.

'You're not trying to wriggle out of this are you?'

'Well, no,' said the archdeacon, in an uncertain voice. 'But I thought it was only supposed to be twice a week. That's how it's always been. Tuesdays and Thursdays.'

The chairman rose from his seat and regarded the archdeacon. 'Tuesdays and Thursdays are no longer enough,' he announced. 'You'll be expected to come in tomorrow, and the next day, and every day after that. There can be no backing out now. It was all agreed at the last meeting.'

'Oh dear,' said the archdeacon, bowing his head. 'I can't have been listening properly.'

The chairman looked at me and nodded slowly. I placed my arm around the archdeacon's shoulder to offer some comfort.

'But that's always been your trouble, hasn't it Norman?' I said. 'You never listen. Not properly.'

only when the sun shines brightly

For a long time I lived beside a railway viaduct that took the trains past my house at rooftop level. It was a brick structure almost a quarter mile in length, and ran along the far side of our street. This being a busy commercial district, the rail-freight company had at some date closed up the supporting arches and let them out as business premises. Some spaces were rented by wholesalers who used them for warehousing. Others had been converted into workshops. The one opposite me was presently occupied by a joiner called Nesbitt. It was a noisy place, with lathes and power-saws going at all hours of the day, augmented every now and then by the trains trundling overhead. A locomotive pulling a heavy load could make all the buildings vibrate as it went past, but fortunately the line was only used for shunting and therefore traffic was infrequent. To tell the truth, I quite liked all the coming and going. It was nice arriving home in the afternoon and seeing the joiner's shop in full swing, especially when Nesbitt had a big job underway. On these occasions there would be staircases or window sashes leaning on the outside wall awaiting collection, while he and his two assistants busily prepared the next piece. One of these helpers was a youth who was supposed to be serving an apprenticeship, but seemed actually to spend most of his time sweeping up wood shavings. The other was an old hand called Stanley. Nesbitt's business methods appeared at first glance chaotic, as he tended to write down his estimates on used envelopes which he then inevitably lost, but the fact that he always had plenty of work was testimony to his basic abilities. I used to go over to the workshop sometimes and have a cup of tea with the three of them. Most days, however, I just gave a cheery wave as I passed by.

Early one morning at the beginning of autumn I heard an odd sound coming from outside. At first I thought I'd been woken by the first shunter of the day, which generally went down the line about five-thirty. This struck me as unusual because I'd become quite accustomed to all the din and could ordinarily sleep through anything. I lay listening for a few moments, and soon realised that it wasn't a train I'd heard. Instead, there came from the direction of the viaduct an irregular flapping noise, as of great wings been beaten. A bit of a breeze seemed to have got up during the night, which was nothing unusual at this time of year, and whenever a gust battered against my window the flapping became more noticeable. Yet for some reason I still couldn't think what might be causing it.

Eventually I decided it was time to get up, so I dressed and opened the blinds. It was barely daylight, but I couldn't help seeing an enormous plastic sheet caught up on the viaduct wall above Nesbitt's workshop. Somehow it had become entangled in the iron railing that ran along the top of the wall, and now hung outstretched in the breeze like some great flag.

I wondered where on earth it could have come from. Pieces of debris quite often came flying in as the autumn equinox took hold, items such as polythene bin-liners and carrier bags, but never had anything as big as this arrived. It was a piece of industrial wrapping, possibly twenty square yards in area, and I assumed it must have come adrift from the back of some lorry or goods truck. All the same, it must have been a strong wind to lift such a bit of flotsam into the air and carry it here. As I made myself a pot of tea I vaguely wondered what Nesbitt would have to say on the matter.

'It'll work itself free after a while,' he announced, as we stood looking up at the plastic sheet later that morning. 'Then we'll get hold of it and put it to some use.'

only when the sun shines brightly

Nesbitt was forever talking about 'putting things to some use'. Quite often he could be observed peering into a builder's skip and pulling out some object that took his fancy, for example, a barrow that had been discarded because it had no wheel, or an empty cable drum. As a result, his workshop was piled in the corners with junk which he'd decided might come in handy at some future time. It appeared now that he'd seen a possible use for this huge plastic sheet, and as soon as he could get his hands on it, he would claim it for his own.

Unfortunately, getting his hands on it was more difficult than he foresaw. When I came home that afternoon the sheet had failed to free itself from the railings, and if anything seemed to have become fixed even more firmly than before. The weather had been deteriorating all day as the wind increased into a minor gale, and the flapping noise had grown louder and more insistent. Drawing near, I saw that Nesbitt now had a ladder against the viaduct wall, and had sent up his apprentice to seize the prize. The ladder, though, was nowhere near long enough for the task, and as the hapless youth poked desperately with a broom handle he looked as though he was going to lose his balance at any minute.

Nesbitt's other assistant, Stanley, had taken the opportunity to stop working and watch this bit of 'sport' from the workshop doorway, and as I approached he gave me a sidelong wink.

'He'll never get that down,' he murmured quietly. 'Not in a month of Sundays.'

'Why doesn't he go to the end of the viaduct and walk back along?' I suggested.

'It's railway property, isn't it?' he replied. 'No one's allowed up there.'

Meanwhile, Nesbitt was losing patience with his apprentice's efforts.

'Try and reach up a bit more!' he kept shouting, which only seemed to make the lad look even more unsteady.

'Notice he doesn't go up there himself?' remarked Stanley, before sidling back to his workbench.

'Come down then!' yelled Nesbitt, before turning to me. 'Useless, young lads are these days. Flaming useless.'

I thought for a moment that he was going to give his apprentice a clip round the ear for his troubles, but after he'd carefully descended they simply took down the ladder and put it away. Next thing Nesbitt and Co. were back at work on their latest joinery project, and appeared temporarily to have given up with the salvage attempt. Nonetheless, the presence of the plastic sheet was difficult to ignore. From inside my house I could hear a constant succession of flapping, whacking and flogging noises, and as the hours passed the racket worsened progressively. I knew, however, that I could do nothing about it, so I closed the blinds, put the kettle on, and had a cup of tea. Before coming in I'd noticed large drops of moisture in the gathering dusk. Soon afterwards it was raining cats and dogs, the drainpipes were flowing at full pelt, and I realized that autumn was now well and truly with us.

*

One of Aesop's Fables tells the story of a wager between the sun and the wind to see which can succeed in removing a traveller's heavy coat. The wind tries first, but however hard it blows it fails to make any headway because the traveller simply buttons his coat even tighter than before. Only when the sun shines brightly does he finally remove it, and the wind roars away in a bad temper.

I was reminded of this fable several times over the next few days, as the wind seemed to be equally unsuccessful with our plastic sheet. It blew like fury for half a week, but the sheet remained firmly attached to the top of the viaduct. Occasionally it became trapped in the railings at more than one point, bellying out and filling with rainwater which would then be released at unexpected times over Nesbitt's doorway. At one such instance the poor fellow was standing directly underneath when it emptied its heavy load, drenching him from head to foot.

I soon noticed that Nesbitt no long regarded the plastic sheet as a 'lucky find', but instead glared up at it balefully for long moments as he tried to work out how to get it down. One afternoon I saw him trying to catch at it with a crude grappling hook on the end of a rope, assisted by Stanley and the young apprentice. Each of them tried and tried again to throw the hook up and get a grip, but they failed every time and had to move quickly out of the way as it came plummeting back down.

'Why don't you write to the rail company?' I suggested.

'They'll be able to get at it easily.'

'Yes, you're right,' replied Nesbitt. 'I think I will.'

However, I knew for a fact that he wouldn't. Nesbitt wasn't the kind of man to spend time writing off letters to railway companies. He had a business to run on a day-to-day basis, and the plastic sheet was really nothing more than an irritating diversion. He would repeatedly claim to be 'doing something about it', but his efforts amounted to nothing more than vain assaults with a grappling hook. Meanwhile, I suspected that Stanley found the whole episode thoroughly entertaining. As for me, well I was beginning slowly to get used to the plastic sheet. I would fall asleep at night to the sound of it whacking and flapping against the viaduct wall, and wake up in the morning to the same thing. It was rapidly becoming part of the scenery, the first object I laid eyes on when I opened my blinds, and I soon learned to live with it. Whenever friends arrived at my front door they would pass comment on the 'eyesore' dangling from the viaduct, suggesting that it lowered the tone of the neighbourhood.

I countered such remarks by pointing at all the everyday litter blowing along the street.

'We live in an untidy world,' I would declare in a glib sort of way. 'You've got to expect a certain amount of industrial detritus in a district like this.'

Judging by the looks on their faces, my friends seemed to find my argument spurious, to say the least.

*

One blustery day a month or so later, a small diesel locomotive chugged slowly along the railway viaduct, paused above Nesbitt's workshop, and then continued on its way. A minute later it came reversing back to where the plastic sheet still lay trapped. A door in the driver's cab slid open, and three men climbed out, all wearing orange fluorescent jackets. They peered over the railing at the sheet as it flogged in the damp breeze, and then began disentangling it. After

37

a while Nesbitt emerged and stood in the street offering words of encouragement. At least, that was what they sounded like from where I watched at my window. It took the three men almost ten minutes to gather the sheet in and fold it up. Then, when they'd exchanged greetings with Nesbitt, they climbed back into their cab and moved off, taking the plastic sheet with them.

That night our street seemed very quiet indeed, and it took me a long time to get to sleep.

At Your Service

My friend Mr Wee was only five feet tall, so if he ever had any domestic chores that required a bit more 'height' I used to go round and help out. If I was lucky he cooked me Chinese food as a reward. If not (which was more often the case) I got tea and burnt toast. Mr Wee's manner was imperious to say the least, but in spite of this the pair of us generally got on very well together.

One day he summoned me to his flat and ordered me to bring my bowsaw.

'There is a tree obscuring my view,' he told me.

I arrived on Sunday morning and removed my boots (a prerequisite for entry into the Wee household on account of his spotless carpets). Then I knocked and waited. There was no answer. I knocked again, and after another minute the door opened. Mr Wee examined my feet and ushered me inside without apologising for the delay.

'I was just bathing the cats.'

As we passed through the hallway I saw his two cats glaring at me from the bathroom, their Sunday morning treat having been temporally interrupted. They were yet to be rinsed, so I continued my wait in the lounge. The gramophone played Beethoven, and on the shelves stood marble busts of all the great composers. They watched me in silence as I awaited the return of Mr Wee. Eventually the ablutions were completed and he came back, sat down and lit his pipe.

The tree in question was outside the rear window (Mr Wee lived on the second floor). It was a great overgrown thorny thing, and he expected me to climb into it and remove some branches. I asked if we were allowed to do this.

'Of course,' he snapped with a note of impatience. 'I've spoken to the property manager.'

'We'll need a ladder,' I said.

'Of course.'

Apparently it was all arranged: we were to carry the (borrowed) ladder through a ground floor flat belonging to one of Mr Wee's neighbours. I wasn't sure if I liked the sound of this, but decided to say nothing. I got my boots back on and we collected the ladder. Then we went to the other flat.

'Shall I take my boots off again?' I asked.

'No,' he replied. 'She won't mind.'

He knocked on the door and it was opened by an elderly lady. This was Mrs Petrov.

'We're coming through with the ladder,' announced Mr Wee.

'But it's Sunday morning,' she protested, in a strong Polish accent.

He ignored her and bustled into the flat, taking the ladder

with him. Mrs Petrov followed and closed the door. I remained outside, waiting. Presently I heard raised voices within. Suddenly the door was flung open and Mrs Petrov commanded me to come and help immediately. I dashed into the flat and found Mr Wee disentangling the ladder from her kitchen curtains. She began shouting at him. He shouted back at her. Then she noticed my boots and shouted at me. Quickly I got the ladder out through the back door.

Some moments later Mr Wee emerged and the two of us started to examine the tree. I remarked that it was going to be a bit of a balancing act and I was likely to get thorns stuck in me. This did not concern him.

'Are you afraid of heights?' he asked.

I said I was not, and started up the ladder. As I did so I noticed curtains beginning to twitch in another of the flats. Feeling very uneasy I continued climbing. Then a man appeared looking rather upset.

'What are you doing?' he demanded of Mr Wee.

'This tree is obscuring my view,' came the reply.

'But you're treading all over my garden!'

Mr Wee looked down at some crushed flowers beneath his feet. He muttered something and led the poor fellow away. I stayed in the tree.

Hearing no more raised voices I commenced work, choosing the largest branch that could be safely removed with a bowsaw. After much sweat and toil, it dropped neatly to the ground.

Mr Wee came back and peered up into the foliage.

'Not that branch: *that* one!' he roared, pointing to a large and almost vertical bough.

'I can't cut that!' I yelled back. 'I'll probably kill myself or put it through someone's window!'

Mr Wee stamped round in a fury while I sawed away at a few other branches until we'd both calmed down a bit. Then I descended. He looked at the finished job and said he 'supposed' that would have to do.

Running the gauntlet of Mrs Petrov again, we returned to his flat. I pointed out that his view was no longer obstructed. In fact, so much light was flooding into the room that Mr Wee decided to close the curtains, thus defeating the object of the exercise.

He grudgingly offered to make me a cup of tea for my troubles, but on this occasion there was to be no Chinese food.

Hark the Herald

The narrow stairway had a wooden banister on each side, and was carpeted in red. I came down five steps, turned at a small landing, and stopped to examine a barometer on the wall. There were five more steps below me. He was waiting at the bottom.

'Morning, sir,' he said. 'Did you manage to get a good night's sleep?'

'Oh, morning,' I replied. 'Er...not quite, actually.'

'I'm very sorry to hear that, sir. Any particular reason?'

'Well, it's just that the merrymaking seemed to go on for a bit too long.'

'Merrymaking, sir?'

'Yes.'

'What sort of merrymaking?'

'I could hear all this laughing and singing. It kept me awake.'

'That's very odd, sir,' he said. 'None of the other guests have mentioned it.'

'Oh…haven't they?'

'No, they haven't. There's been no one complaining about any "merrymaking".'

'Oh no, I'm not complaining,' I said quickly. 'It's just that I thought it went on a bit too long, that's all.'

His name was Mr Sedgefield. I'd met him late the previous evening when I first arrived, and he had put me in their 'best single room'. Now he gave me a long, thoughtful look before speaking again. 'Well we don't want your Christmas spoilt, sir, so we'll have to look into the matter.'

'Thanks.'

He remained at the foot of the stairs gazing up at me, and for the first time I noticed he was wearing a kitchen apron emblazoned with a smiling pink pig. I felt unable to continue my descent until he'd moved out of the way, but he showed no inclination to do this so I turned my attention once again to the barometer.

'I see the pressure's fallen overnight.'

'Yes,' he said. 'Should make for some very interesting seas during the next day or two.'

'That's what I was thinking. Might be nice to have a stroll along the clifftops later.'

'If only we'd known your plans earlier, sir. You could have gone with the others. A whole party of them left not half an hour ago.'

'What, without breakfast?'

'Oh no, we made sure they all had breakfast first.'

'Does that mean I'm too late?'

'Of course not,' he said, stepping back at last and indicating the dining room. 'You might have missed the bacon and eggs, but we can always rustle up some porridge.'

I heard myself thanking him once again, and then continued my way downstairs. A large upright clock in the hall showed that it was five past nine. This didn't strike me as an unduly late time to be coming down for breakfast in a guest house, but it was obvious that everyone else had already been and gone. All the tables in the dining room were bare apart from a small one in the corner by the window. This had cup, saucer and cutlery set for one.

Mr Sedgefield ushered me towards it and I sat down just as another man appeared in the doorway and said, 'Sugar, honey or treacle?'

'Pardon?' I asked.

'In your porridge.'

'Oh, sorry. Er...treacle, please, if you've got it.'

This second man also wore a kitchen apron, but his depicted a laughing cow rather than a smiling pig.

'Righto,' he said, and next moment was gone again.

'Years since I've had porridge with treacle in it,' I remarked to Mr Sedgefield.

'Yes,' he replied. 'We have things here you can't often get in other parts of the country.'

'Actually, I didn't mean...,' I began, but now he too had left the dining room.

In the last few moments he'd discreetly placed a small coffee pot on the table, so I poured myself a cup and took the opportunity to glance at my surroundings. The walls were arrayed with paintings and framed photographs of maritime scenes, past and present. In one picture an ocean liner with red funnels departed from some great international port. In the next, a fishing smack unloaded at the quay. There were yachts in black and white 'going to windward off Portland Bill', and others in colour with their spinnakers billowing. Meanwhile, ancient triremes prepared for battle in the Aegean. The nautical decor had been made festive with berries, and seasonal greenery, but it was overdone somewhat, so that the Victory at Trafalgar now lay partially obscured by sprigs of holly. I'd seen the same sort of thing in the hallway when I arrived. Every attempt had been made to give the place a 'yuletide' feel, but behind the mistletoe and the tinsel there were always icebergs and distant lightships. It was the costal setting that did it. This was a seaside guest house that catered mainly for summer visitors, and it was decked out according to their expectations.

Yet the place had its attractions in mid-winter too, which was why I'd decided to spend Christmas here. Through the window I could see a silver gleam where the sky and the sea reflected one another. A perfect place for getting the New Year off to an optimistic start.

The house stood on the clifftops above a cove. It had been built to withstand the extremities of weather, and although there were two storeys it was very squat and low. Hence the staircase with only ten steps. The rooms were small, and staying here somehow reminded me of being on board a ship. I'd arrived late the night before, when the place was in darkness. Mr Sedgefield had let me in and attended to everything, but I had been aware of someone else's presence in the kitchen at the end of the hall. Presumably this was the man who'd asked me about my porridge. We'd had a bit of a chat about the weather, during which I'd learnt that we were 'too far west' to get any snow in 'normal years'. Then I was given a mince pie and a glass of sherry before going up to bed.

I had hoped to be lulled straight to sleep by the sound of waves gently breaking on the seashore. Instead,

I'd been kept awake for some time by all this laughing and singing. I couldn't tell what part of the house it was coming from, but it seemed to continue until the early hours. There were glasses tinkling as well.

Now I had no objection to people enjoying themselves. After all, it was Christmas, the season of goodwill, and they were only having a little harmless fun. I just thought it went on for a bit too long really, so I resolved to mention it to Mr Sedgefield when I saw him in the morning. Finally, the merrymaking ceased and I slept at last, but I was so exhausted that I failed to wake until almost nine o'clock, and there was only porridge left for breakfast.

*

The treacle had been poured over the top, but I was allowed to stir it in myself. Meanwhile, Mr Sedgefield hovered around the dining room and ensured that my coffee cup was replenished frequently. I had to admit that the service was excellent, although he did tend to fuss a little.

After a while he said, 'Don't mind me asking sir, but did you have any plans for this evening?'

'Not really,' I answered.

'Well, if you're interested, some of the other guests are having a bit of a Christmas get together later on.'

'Oh right.'

'There'll be games like snake-and-ladders, charades and blind man's buff, as well as mince pies for everyone.'

'Sounds like fun.'

'Yes, indeed,' he said. 'And I'm sure they'd love you to join them.'

'Well, yes.' I replied. 'I'd be very glad to.'

'After supper then, in the reception room?'

'Right, I'll be there.'

'Good.' A moment passed, and then he asked, 'Porridge, alright, was it?'

'Delicious, thanks,' I said.

'It's a shame you had to miss the full breakfast, but of course you will be entitled to a packed lunch.'

'When?'

'When you go out.'

'Oh…er, OK thanks.'

'You will be going out, won't you, sir?'

'Well, I hadn't definitely decided, but, yes I expect I most probably will.'

'There are some fine walks to be had on the cliffs,' he announced. 'And if you're feeling particularly robust, I can strongly recommend the view at Temple Point.'

I wasn't feeling 'particularly robust' after my

sleepless night, but it was clear that my host wanted me out for the day. Presumably this was so preparations could be made for the coming evening, and therefore I obliged him by agreeing that I would indeed be going for a walk later. Next thing he'd produced a map, which he opened and spread before me on the table.

'With a bit of luck you'll meet the other guests somewhere en route,' he said. 'I gather they're heading in the same direction.'

Temple Point turned out to be a spit of land protruding into the sea about four miles away to the west. Obviously Mr Sedgefield had more in mind for me than a casual seaside stroll, but by the time he'd indicated the waymarked paths and other suggested viewpoints I'd come fully to accept the idea. Besides, I thought, it would give me a good appetite for supper.

An hour later I was in the hallway putting on my boots when he emerged from the kitchen.

'We're just doing your sandwiches now, sir. Cheese be all right, will it?'

'Yes, fine thanks.'

'Like an apple as well?'

'Please.'

'Right you are.'

He disappeared again, and for the next few moments I heard lowered voices speaking in the kitchen. Not wanting to eavesdrop on their conversation I stepped out into the porch, closing the front door behind me. In the corner stood a large Christmas tree. It was decorated with fairy lights, and as I waited I noticed them flicker a couple of times. Thinking there must be a loose bulb somewhere I began working round the tree, testing each one. I'd got about halfway when the door opened and Mr Sedgefield came out.

'Something wrong, sir?' he asked.

'Well,' I replied. 'There seems to be a fault somewhere. I was just looking for it.'

'Now don't you go worrying about that,' he said. 'You're suppose to be on holiday so just let me deal with any problems.'

'Oh…OK then.'

'Here you are.' He handed me a neat package in a greaseproof paper bag. The clock in the hallway struck eleven. It was time for me to go.

'By the way,' I asked. 'What time's supper?'

'Whenever you like, sir,' he replied. 'Just take as long as you wish.'

*

The guest house was bounded on one side by a garden with ornamental trees and shrubs, including several rhododendrons. Behind it towards the sea lay open countryside, small fields with sparse hedges that gave out to tracts of bracken near the edge of the cliffs. I found the waymarked path and headed west.

The weather was mild but, because of the overnight

drop in pressure, decidedly blustery. It also accounted for the 'interesting seas' that Mr Sedgefield had mentioned. The whole ocean seemed to be mounting a headlong charge against this stretch of the coast, with huge breakers crashing against the cliffs below. Not that I was complaining, of course. It was just this sort of wild bleakness that I'd come looking for. I walked with my head down in the wind, stopping from time to time to watch seabirds performing acrobatics above the waves. In one of the fields some cows stood huddled with their backs to the sea, nudging at a bale of hay that had been laid out for them. Here and there in the distance I could see occasional low buildings, some of which I took to be farmhouses, others I supposed were holiday homes to rent. What I didn't see, though, were people. No one else had chosen to walk the coastal path today, and there was no sign of Mr Sedgefield's other guests. Maybe they'd gone in the opposite direction.

It was mid afternoon when I finally arrived at

Hark the Herald

Temple Point. Here the cliffs had broken away to leave a great towering arch of rock, pounded on all sides by the white swirling waters and resembling some great piece of gothic architecture. I clambered right to the end of the promontory, and than sat looking across at the arch. Every now and then a shower of spray would rise up from below, momentarily threatening to engulf me before subsiding again. Meanwhile the soaring columns of rock stood immobile and unmoved by the surging waves. It was a marvellous sight.

I spent quite a while gazing out and pondering what primeval forces had conspired together to create such a place. Then I ate my sandwiches.

*

Darkness had fallen by the time I arrived back at the guest house, but surprisingly there was no sign of activity inside. This came as a bit of a disappointment. The walk home from Temple Point had seemed to take much longer than the outward journey, with the threat of rain coming in later, and I'd begun to look forward to a little Christmas cheer.

The get together that Mr Sedgefield had spoken of now appeared most attractive. I could just imagine him and his partner fussing around in the reception room, lighting a log fire and preparing some fine mulled wine. Or perhaps roasting chestnuts. It would also be a chance at last to meet the other guests.

As it was, I came up the garden path to find the place silent and gloomy. Even the fairy lights in the porch had given up flickering and seemed finally to have gone out altogether. Before going inside I decided to complete my test on the bulbs. There were half a dozen left to do, and when I got to the last one I discovered it was loose.

I gave it the necessary twist and all the lights were restored.

Then I knocked on the door and waited.

A minute passed before Mr Sedgefield opened up.

'Ah,' he said. He was no longer wearing his apron.

'Ah,' I replied with a grin. 'I'm back.'

'Yes.'

I was led inside and we stood for a few awkward moments in the hall.

'Not too late for supper am I ?' As I spoke I realised my appetite had returned with a vengeance. I felt quite hungry again.

'Well,' he said. 'I suppose we could do a cold plate at a push.'

'Is that what the others are having ?'

'The others had theirs hours ago.'

'Oh…did they ?'

'Indeed they did, I'm sorry to say you've missed them again.'

'How ?'

'They've gone carol-singing. Shame really, you could have gone with them.'

'But what about the get together ?'

'I'm afraid that's postponed.'

He showed me into the reception room, and then went off to the kitchen. There were no logs burning in the grate, only an electric fire with one bar switched on. And there were no decorations. When Mr Sedgefield finally returned he brought a plate with some cold pork, a few slices of bread and butter, and some pickle.

'Bon appetit,' he said.

I watched as he went to the dresser and opened a sherry bottle, pouring out three glasses. He gave one to me, and then carried the other two out of the room. He didn't come back.

The evening passed very slowly. I finished my supper and

spent a while looking at some National Geographic magazines. There was enough sherry left in the bottle for another glass or two, but I was unwilling to help myself without asking. So at about half past ten I went up to my room.

I sat on the bed and listened. At any moment I hoped to hear the sound of merrymakers returning, followed soon afterwards by glasses tinkling and joyous voices calling me down to be with them.

Yet all I heard was the murmuring sea as it broke against the shore.

the End

Also by Magnus Mills:

The Restraint of Beasts

All Quiet on the Orient Express

Three To See The King

once in a blue moon

The Scheme for Full Employment

The Scheme for Full Employment

'I've been having a look at your daily mileage reports for December. According to this you did sixty-three miles on Wednesday the fourth, sixty-three miles on Thursday the fifth, and on Friday the sixth, one million, twelve thousand and twenty-two miles. Where did you go that day?'

The Scheme for Full Employment
is a wonderfully original fable - and a modern classic
in the making.

'He has no literary precedent, and he also appears to have no imitators. He mines a seam that no one else touches upon, every sentence in every book having a Magnus Mills ring to it that no other writer could produce.'
- The Independent.

Published by Harper Collins

Magnus Mills' second collection of short stories:

once in a blue moon

is also available from acorn book company:

My mother's house was under siege. One chill Friday evening in November I arrived to find the entire neighbourhood in a state of high alert. The police had blocked the street at both ends. A helicopter was circling overhead, and there were snipers hidden in the garden.

'Get down!' they hissed, when I approached.

'It's OK,' I replied. 'I've been on this case right from the beginning.'

ISBN 0-9544959-0-X
£5.99

Something else by Magnus Mills...

In a league of his own

He was the most talented footballer ever to emerge from the Great Continent. A genius with the ball, he made his first appearance representing a tiny republic in an international competition. His popularity was instant. Under the gaze of the world's television cameras he won many admirers with his sheer flair and exuberance, not to mention three spectacular goals. He also attracted the attention of the big clubs, and soon received lucrative offers to move abroad. Success at the top level brought yet more acclaim. He was seen as a true sportsman. His personal conduct on the field of play was without parallel and during a long and sparkling career his name became a byword for all that was good in the game. On retirement he returned home to coach the national side, enjoying further triumphs in his new role. Later he was appointed Minister for Sport. Eventually he became President of his country, and ruled with a rod of iron for thirty years.

All our titles are available direct from

acorn book company
PO Box 191, Tadworth
Surrey KT20 5YQ

POST FREE IN THE UK

Cheques payable to acorn book company.
or email your order to sales@acornbook.co.uk